For Maame Ama Fosua & Maame Esi Kumwa —L.O.

For my daughter, Lavanda —L.L.

Library of Congress Control Number: 2021951683
ISBN 978-0-06-301576-0
The artist used acrylic paint, cut paper, and tissue paper to create the illustrations for this book.

Typography by Chelsea C. Donaldson
22 23 24 25 26 RTLO 10 9 8 7 6 5 4 3 2 1
❖
First Edition

BLACK GOLD

by Laura Obuobi

illustrations by London Ladd

HARPER
An Imprint of HarperCollinsPublishers

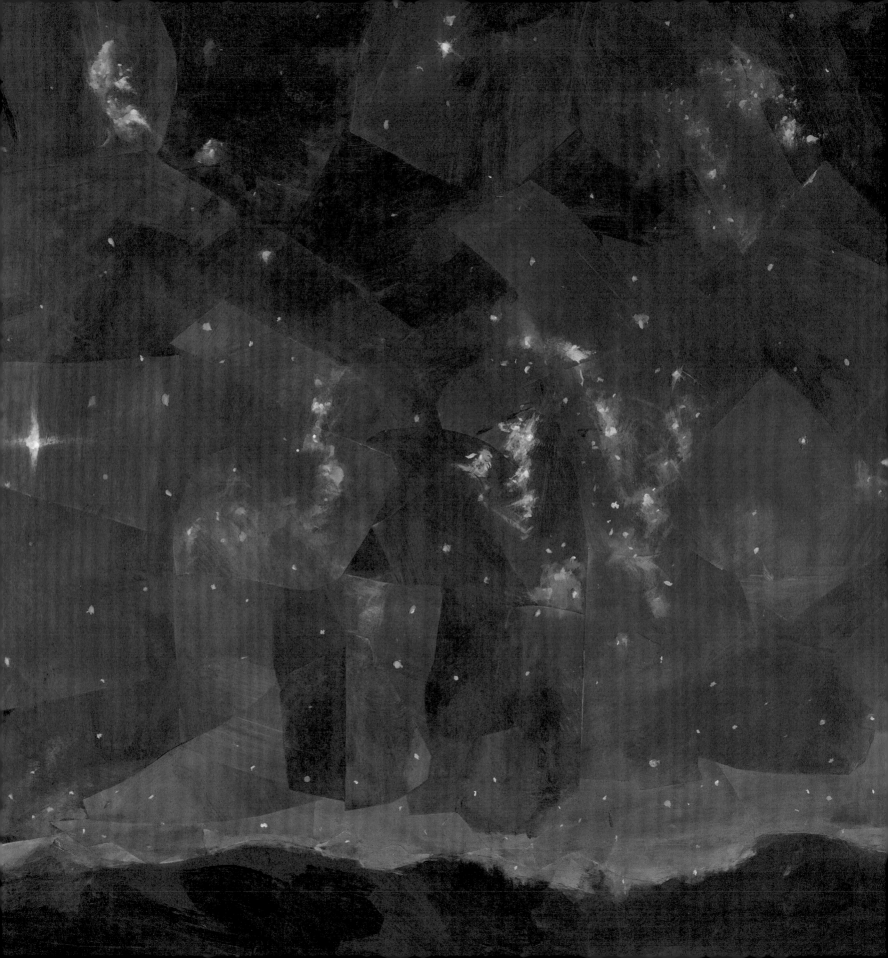

When the Universe decided to create you,
she drew you from the earth—
rich,
dark,
and full of everything that gives life.

She reached deep into the ground and scooped you.
With her hands, she formed and molded your body.

She hardened bones to give you shape
and softened your heart and lungs
to flex to the beat of their own drum.

She smoothed your skin,
lengthened your limbs,
and gently shaped your head.

She sloped your nose,
teased out your ears,
and carefully placed your brows.

She adorned you with eyes
like black star sapphires and
gifted you with full lips
to speak your truth.

With her palms, she rubbed your scalp.
Your hair coiled around her fingers,
stretched up to heaven, and
touched the feet of her throne.

She reached into a river,
collecting pellets of gold.

She crushed them, forming three piles of gold dust.

The Universe rubbed the first pile all over you,
spun the second pile into gold threads, wove it into cloth,
and swaddled you with it.

She molded the third pile into a wreath of roses
and crowned your curls with it.

Then the Universe breathed in

and breathed out.

Her power hovered around you.

You breathed in.

Her power flowed into you.

You breathed out.

Alive!

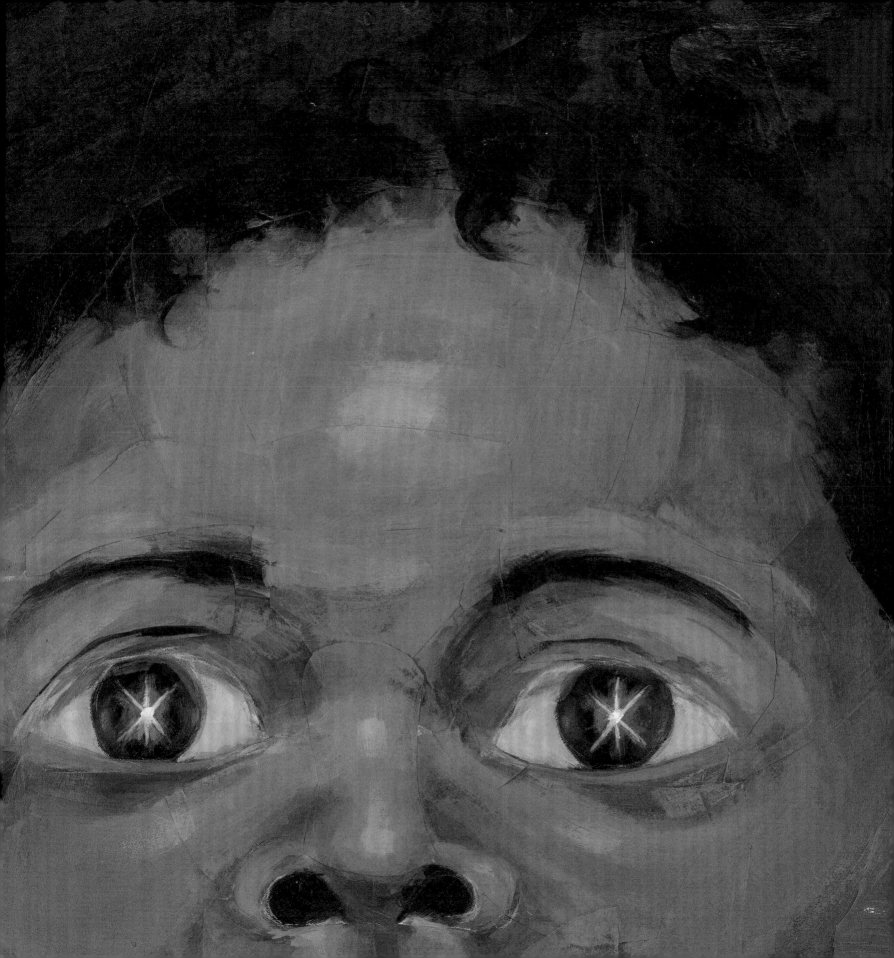

But her work was not finished yet.
The Universe passed you over to the Sun,
who filled you with light.

The Sun passed you over to the Moon,

who filled you with wisdom.

Then the Universe wrapped her arms around you,
filling you with love.

Her work was complete.

When they ask where you come from, tell them, "I am from a place that is rich, dark, and full of everything that gives life. I was kissed by the Sun, cradled by the Moon, and wrapped in love."

"I am a child of the Universe.

I am Black Gold."